The Destiny Thief

by Stephen Taylor

Many thanks to all those who have supported me over the last years. Special thanks to my family and close friends for their support and belief in me when I felt there was nothing left to give. Also thanks to Red Deer Writers Ink and John Burnham for their critique and encouragement.

Thanks to Sir Terry Pratchett for following his imagination;
I am one of the many he inspired to do the same.

For all those who have made difficult decisions; thank you for being brave.

#

Cover photo by Alexandru Zdrobău on Unsplash.com

Prologue

A breath lingers. It swallows deep. A satisfied smile returning to sleep. A morning ritual not undone for a hundred years has kept pacified The Great One. Her brimstone breath buried under darkness. Powerful majesty tempered by sloth and sacrifice. Worshipped and feared by the few who know of her, a world unaware strewn about.

But if she were to wake...
If she were to stir...

Chapter One

Lisa and Kari Williams begin this fine mid-summers day like most others. The fraternal twins walk through early morning streets to their favourite cafe, eager for breakfast and conversation before the bustle of the city begins in earnest. A place of magic, warriors, and adventure; there is always something happening to stir the imagination in the river city of Adayr.

As they stroll down pristine streets, Lisa talks about the latest book she is reading; hands and loose blonde hair expressing her exuberance as she retells the story to Kari. Kari is politely listening, but her mind is already planning out the rest of her day. She can't wait to explore the fields just west of the city, ride their horses, and climb the nearby cliffs.

Westport is the wealthy section of Adayr, and the region of the city the girls have called home their whole lives. Built upon hills located on the western shore of Lennenden River, it avoids the majority of sights and smells spread by the general populace across the bridge.

The Williams sisters are well known in this part of town. Their father raised them alone while also achieving the position of Adayr's chief lawyer: becoming largely responsible for passing the rules and regulations that have helped make the city as safe as it is. Because of his position they have enjoyed the very best the world has to offer. A large home, incredible food, many servants, excellent education, and unlimited recreation. Their seventeen years have been well spent.

Arriving at the cafe there is a table waiting for them at their favourite spot outside. Such prestigious regulars are accordingly pandered to. Upon seeing them approach a waiter immediately makes his way from the counter and helps them to their seats, "The usual today, Ms. Williams?" A simple smiling nod from Lisa and he heads back inside as she continues her conversation, "...and, you just don't see it coming! The mountains explode and turn into giants! Then Greggor has to protect the city from not one...but two armies! And only armed with a magic cutlass! It's so intense! I almost can't bring myself to finish it!"

"Sure Lisa," Kari leans back in her chair, brushing her dark hair behind her ear, "very intense. But what about the real world? Don't you ever want to just get out there and explore? Find out what's beyond the forests of the north? What's really inside the mountains?"

"Kari, we both know what's in the forests. It's much safer to read about adventure. Looking for it just gets you in trouble. As you know."

"Yeah, but it's fun." She grins, "People make boundaries and rules for safety, but if you want to explore you've got to step outside of those things. Take a risk."

Lisa knows her sister's comment is a half-bluff. As adventurous as she is they both share the same aversion to the sights and smells they occasionally experience from the city proper.

Being regulars the chef had prepared their food before they even got there; the waiter returns with their coffee and exquisitely prepared breakfasts as Lisa responds to her sister, "No thanks, I'll live vicariously through Greggor for now. Slaying monsters and exploring new places is just so...well...you know." She points with her butter knife toward Adayr, "Just...not romantic at all in real life. Stinky. But not romantic."

#

Everett Brennem staggers from the tavern; drool, spittle, and the remnants of an impressive number of pints reflecting the early morning sunlight off his unkempt beard. Having stayed up the whole night celebrating, he bids farewell to his new and equally inebriated friends. The drinks have been on him all night, as he revelled in the riches that poured in the previous day.

Having heard of the great city of Adayr, the young merchant had ridden horse and buggy for days; eager to sell his own special brand of magical equipment to the men and women that frequent this rancid, bustling, metropolis. Adayr had delivered in spades with his entire cart selling in a matter of hours. All he had to do was what any merchant would have done in his situation: lie through his teeth.

The truth is he didn't have any magical items. And he wouldn't want to be around any even if he had the chance - way too finicky to be dealing with. On the other hand he learned that any item can be greatly increased in market value just by putting the word 'magical' in front of it. So he sold magical pots, magical pans, magical knives, and magical boots. Even his magical cart was bought by an excitable group of adventurers.

There are rules though. Very important rules to be remembered by every trader that chooses to operate here. And he now wrestles against the grogginess, attempting to remember what they are.

"Numb...number...nu...wun!" he mutters to himself, "Dun...don lie 'bou watch...watcher got." He giggles a little as he distinctly remembers breaking that rule. Very much on purpose.

"Too!" He points a finger to the sky, mimicking the wisened man who had given him the rundown before he arrived, "Ifs yer gon...lie! Meks...*hic*...mekshure deys nogon finds yeraft...after.

"Deys gorbee...ded. OR...OR...OOOOOORRRRRRR..." He falls against the wall of the tavern, briefly admiring the layers of patterned vomit that have accrued over the years before adding his own contribution. Wiping his mouth and shaking his head he continues, "Ooooooooorrrrrrr.....? Huh. Or...or. Or." Sudden realisation accelerates the sobering process, "Ooooooooh bugger."

The rules are simple, and passed eagerly from one merchant to the next. Adayr is quite unique in that it caters almost exclusively to adventurers. These adventurers come here to experience the natural world that surrounds this city on the frontier of humanity.

What is largely out in the forests, hills, and mountains that surround, are orcs. There are many other monsters and creatures out there, but the often bear-sized, humanoid, green skinned, and tusked monsters are the most common prize sought after. There is a good trade in price for orc carcasses in the city and so warriors and adventurers come here from all walks of life attempting to become rich as they bask in the fame of true heroism.

In an environment such as this, it is often a risky thing to be a merchant. Those who are not satisfied with their goods will at the very least, in one way or another, make it painfully clear to you. And so the rules for selling things here are simple.

One. Do not lie about what you are selling. Especially if you are selling magical potions or equipment. Do not even try to talk it up. Only sell what you actually have. As has been made clear, Everett quite willingly broke this rule and made quite the killing because of it. Selling random equipment and drinks as magical artifacts and potions increases their value exponentially. And that is why there is rule number two.

Two. If you lie about what you have, make sure they won't be able to find you after. This is the route the occasional merchant chooses to take. The problem is, this is a one-and-done philosophy. If you lie and they buy and they make it through their quest… you are going to die.

The only option if taking this route is to get out of the city and never come back. Adventurers will rarely chase an errant merchant if they leave. But if they stay…say…overnight to celebrate their earnings…

"Buggerbuggerbuggerbuggerbuggerbugger." Muttering like a clockwork engine and desperately trying to convince his body to cooperate; Master Brennem moves as quickly as possible to where he left his horse. Unfortunately, when he gets to the stable he sees that she is gone. It takes a couple of seconds pondering before Everett remembers selling her as well. He grins, despite his predicament, "Mergshi…Mergical hor….hor…horshey. *Heh*."

Stumbling back outside he begins to make his way to the bridge that crosses Lennenden River and leads to Westport: the wealthy sector of Adayr and possibly a way he can escape before finding himself facing any surviving disgruntled customers.

He manages to sneak a seat on the back of one of the carts that is being wheeled over the bridge to set up in Westport's main square. These buggies are filled with the good stuff: genuine magical artifacts being sold to adventurers who can afford to pay a premium for them. And sometimes to the locals as well. Though they tend to avoid magic if possible, citing a suspicion that being around too much of the stuff for too long drives people crazy. The young merchant is of a differing opinion: he reckons that crazy people tend to be attracted to magical things in the first place.

Hopping off before the driver comes to a full stop, Everett stumbles and falls on his side. Resisting the urge to throw up again he stands to get his bearings. The sun is behind him. That's good.

"Merv…moo…move. Dat way." Legs beginning to cooperate a little better he makes his way up Westport's hills, attempting to exit the city as soon as possible.

His shuffling gate takes him rapidly through the wealthiest part of town, any other day he would have marvelled at the architecture and pristine streets.

There are not many out this early but he does draw the eye of one of two sisters enjoying breakfast outside a cafe, unwittingly sparking a thought to life in her head as he rushes past. The smell that follows him causes both girls to involuntarily scrunch their noses and wait a few seconds before they can enjoy the taste of their rare roast once again.

Lisa has had a different merchant from town on her mind for a while; a thought that has been growing in the back of her head. Kari also noticed that the smell was occupied by a merchant and lets her dark hair frame the slightly sarcastic expression on her face, waiting for Lisa to say what she knows is coming.

"He knows something, Kari, I'm sure of it!" Kari sighs as this weeks-old conversation starts up again, "Knows what, Lisa?"

The waiter makes his way to their table, carefully removing the remains of their breakfasts before gracefully disappearing back inside the small shop.

"I don't know. He just always has a smile on his face. Like he's put one over on the whole world."

"That smile, dear sister, is the smile of a lunatic. He's a crazy old man! He sells relics and magic items to even crazier young men. Magic takes your sanity away eventually; everyone knows that! Forget about him. Let's spend today riding horses."

"I can't...I have to go to market."

"Get a servant to go for you; it's not like we have a shortage of them around the house."

"But..."

"You just want to visit his stall again. And get hit on by the travelling adventurers."

"Okay, that's gross. They're always sweaty, stinky, half-dressed and half magic-crazed. I just want to know what he knows. And maybe we'll find something to buy. Come on, please!"

Kari's eyes couldn't roll any louder, but she grudgingly puts her coffee down and joins Lisa; their conversation adding to the waking populace as they make their way to market down white cobbled streets.

The early morning air is fresh and crisp, a bright summer sun rapidly shortening the shadows about this picturesque city. Adayr's architecture is famed throughout the world. The wealth in trade has attracted many powerful and business-oriented families with they, in turn, bringing the finest tradespeople. The result has been swift over the last hundred years, turning a small port on the wide Lennenden River into the most beautiful and powerful city known to man.

The business of adventure is a lucrative one indeed.

#

Everett continues his hasty drunken shuffle toward the Western Gate, attempting to exit the city before any of his surviving customers make it back to town. This being his first time in Adayr he could be forgiven for thinking his plan of escape was original. The five bloodied and bruised survivors of a quest-party awaiting him at the gate, however, are adamantly choosing to not be in a forgiving mood.

"Bugger."

Everett turns and runs, seeking to lose his pursuers in the

winding streets that litter the hills of Westport. But a drunken visiting merchant has little chance of escaping a group of very angry and very sober adventurers. He is caught in minutes.

Being held off his feet against a wall by a rather large man, Everett experiences a first hand view of several blades being placed into threatening positions about his person. He gulps, fear and adrenaline helping his mind to sober up, "Come on now lads, *urk!* And Miss," he corrects himself as a particularly uncomfortable blade gets even more so, "Lets talk about this. I'm sure we can work something out. Full refunds even." His heart silently dies at such a suggestion, but the circumstance demands extreme measures.

"Full refunds. Y'hear that? He wants to give us full refunds. Six friends dead and he wants to give us our money back."

"Even Geir?"

"Huh?" The leader of the group turns to look at his counterpart.

"Well...Geir...he was a bit of a git really."

"Huh?"

"Y'know, always sneaking extra rations when we weren't looking. And he'd have your gold if you didn't watch it."

"So?"

"Well...my point is he wasn't exactly what I'd call a friend. He was more of...a git."

"And Renny too." The big one that is holding Everett against the wall decides to pipe in, "Not gonna miss that stinky little sod. Never washed his feet. I swear he was trying to grow plant-life between his toes."

The rest of the group murmurs their approval of the aforementioned deceased members being removed from the 'friends list'. Their leader tries to rescue the situation, "Listen. The point we are trying to make, is that this pathetic excuse for a human being sold us dodgy goods. These dodgy goods led to the demise of several members of our party and that is not acceptable."

"What...them being dodgy goods or them killing off our mates?"

"'Cept Geir and Renny."

"Yeah."

"Both! Look. Can we just re-focus on the problem at hand?"

"What problem is that boss?"

"The problem as to which of this conniving little turd's extremities we'll be cutting off first."

The group as one return their attention to the trapped merchant and grin with malicious intent, "Now come on! There has to be a way we can figure this out!"

"Oh there is lad. We're going to figure out a way you don't ever get found. Well. Not in a recognizable fashion anyway."

It is at this moment that a guard patrol turns the corner and comes face to face with the situation at hand. Everett takes full advantage, "Help! Help me! *Gurk!*" A hand closes on his throat. The two guards approach the group and stop at a distance, a bit nervous about the number of potential suspects, "What's going on here? You fellers (and lady) alright this morning? Causing a bit of a fuss for this part of town you know."

"Sorry about the disturbance, Officer," the leader speaks up, "Just taking care of a lying merchant what got my squad murdered."

The look on the guards' faces turns to utter relief, "Oh, well then. Have at it. Just do us a favour and don't off him 'round here. Blood is murder to clean out o' the cobbles."

With that the two men turn and continue their route, a look of utter shock and panic taking place on the captive's face.

The group's leader leans against the wall to explain, "See. 'Round here the punishment for selling fake magic is death. The higher up's don't like having this business made more dangerous than it already is, and the guards much prefer if we take care of it ourselves, saves them on the cleanup work,

"You heard the officers, let's get him back across the bridge."

And with that a stunned and pleading young man is dragged back through the streets: desperately praying for deliverance to come from any entity that may be in a slightly good mood.

Chapter Two

It was a morning just like this one.

Just like this one.

Phynel Williams looks out his second floor window in the courthouse, summer sun rising on the river city of Adayr. He takes a moment away from his work to let the sadness and regret rise from his gut as he remembers the last time he saw his wife.

He was holding their twin girls in his arms, just six months old, watching the guard take Julia away. The desperation in her eyes as she fought against them. The desperation in his heart as he fought the urge to save her. So that he could save their daughters.

No one has seen her since. Not even him.

Seventeen years later and the guilt still haunts him, but his heart accepts it. It is his punishment, he reasons, for letting her go. For letting things get that out of hand. For burdening her with the truth.

The rumours are she went crazy. And he is okay to let them think that, it is not far from what happened. One day a normal, loving wife and mother and the next, totally delusional and trying to kidnap her twin daughters. He remembers wondering how he was going to survive without her. All these years later he wonders if he actually did.

Looking out on the city for which he sold his soul, Phynel brings his mind to the present. This is a place of magic and warriors: a fungal mix of adventurers and the markets designed to make them happy. Taverns and bars, women and men, weapons and magic, potions and armour. All to feed the main economy that has been the lifeblood of Adayr since its inception a century ago: orc hunting. These monsters were discovered by the first settlers in the area as they explored the forests and mountains north of what was originally an outpost.

What began as an attempt to eradicate a menace has become an extremely lucrative business with all sorts of people hoping to become famous and prove their might to the world as true heroes. Those more concerned for their physical well being come here to trade and sell. And the truly business-minded make a very lucrative living at the expense of willing human life.

Such a place is in need of law and justice to guide the masses, and as chief lawyer, Phynel has made a name for himself guiding the people of Adayr toward better lives. Long hours and sleepless nights have brought a semblance of peace to what would otherwise be a chaotic and swarthy place. He lets himself feel a sense of pride as he thinks about his accomplishments and the need the city has for a man like him. A man who loves this place almost as much as he loves his daughters. Almost as much as he loved her.

He continues his gaze out the window as Lisa and Kari walk by, heading down to market. Phynel smiles, the gods have truly blessed him with such wonderful daughters. He watches them until they are out of sight, then breathes a deep breath of clean air before returning to the duties awaiting him on the desk.

#

The surrounding farmland is enclosed by hills, forests, and mountains; and within those places are many fantastic creatures. Some benign, some dangerous, and some the stuff of legend. Many believe there are even dragons still hiding in the depths of the earth, though the last one found was killed over forty years ago.

This beautiful and picturesque place feeds its own economy with travelling bards willing to sing about your exploits for the right price (and willing to make something up for a more right price). These fanciful musicians roam the surrounding lands inspiring imagination and placing dreams of glory and wealth in the young.

But those who grew up here are not fooled by the songs or the tales or the merchants. They've seen it all before. And as nice as it is that pest control comes to their city and pays them to be here, it sure would be nice if the streets didn't so often smell of sweat, dung, blood, and beer.

Living in Westport, the twins manage to avoid the majority of unpleasant sights and smells, but every now and then the wind shifts and the girls have to place herbs under their noses to combat the reminder that people can actually smell like that.

It is this rancid odour that is the main reason Kari has no interest in visiting the market today. Even though this particular market is on their side of the river, it still brings them closer to that wafting stench and they still have to see those adventurers wealthy enough to afford what is sold on this side of the bridge. And those adventurers tend to be extra sure of themselves. Because killing a few orcs means that every member of the opposite sex wants you. Of course it does.

Lisa, for some reason, has become fascinated with one ridiculous old man who goes simply by the moniker of 'Rivets'. Every morning he wheels his cart across the bridge from the eastern port and pays for his stall space. And every day he just sits there grinning; magic items laying across his counter with price tags that change every day, depending on what kind of mood he's in. There are always people checking out his goods and a few of them even sell. And they must work because he's been there longer than either of the girls' short seventeen years of life. Either that or they don't work; and they don't work very, very well…

The sisters push their way through the early morning rush, Lisa pulling Kari along by the hand. Marketeers screaming way too loud and being way too confident about the incredible flavours of their food and the incredible powers of their enchanted wares; bards bartering with their clients about 'creative exaggeration' before heading to the streets to sing about the exploits of the previous day.

There are not a few adventurers out this morning, some jovial and planning their next excursion with friends, some making deals, some trying to shake off hangovers, some trying to maintain drunkenness, but all of them eyeing up the market stalls.

Both girls involuntarily find themselves wincing at the odour permeating the square as they push through the sweaty men and women; muscles, leather, chainmail and swords.

Suddenly a disembodied orc head is thrust in Kari's face, "Waddya think, babe? Got this one just yesterday. Want to have a drink with a real life hero?" Behind the disturbingly nightmare inducing green and bloody mess stands a tall, strong, and cocksure man. His armour covers about half of his chest and his arrogant smile about half of his face. Kari throws up a little in her mouth. Ignoring the incredibly romantic gesture, she starts thinking of ways to punish Lisa for this misadventure later on.

Lisa spots Rivets' stall across the square and drags Kari, who just wants to ride her horses, through every sweaty armpit she can find. A voice behind them calls, "Don't worry, your friend can come too if she wants!"

The old man sits behind his wooden cart, manic grin beaming at every onlooker, grey and white hair not quite sure in which direction to grow, piercing green eyes betraying an intelligence lost to the corruption of the magic he trades in. His leather and steel garb covered in pockets, strange contraptions, tools, and rivets. Every now and then he gives a brief chuckle as an adventurer examines a sword or bow, today's price tag hanging from the handle.

The girls walk up, Lisa excited about the day and Kari thinking of sweet, sweet vengeance, "Hi Rivets, what's for sale today?"

Rivets takes his attention away from the woman currently examining a scimitar and grins, "Hi there girls! Lotsa goods goin' fer good prices today! Take a look-see!"

The old man picks up a large broadsword and exuberantly offers it to them. Lisa reads the price tag, "'Sword of Ba Shinge, 5 Gold'...Ba Shinge?"

"Fer bashin' orcs with lass." He chuckles, eyes wide open with glee, "Any sword can slice, but this sword bashes."

"Um. Wouldn't that just mean it's not sharp?" Kari states with accusatory eyebrow raised. The old man chuckles. "Ok,"

Lisa continues gazing around at the display, "...what else do you have?"

Rivets spends the next few minutes trying to sell them different weapons and armour that they would never use or fit into. Bow of De Termination, Axe of Fragments, Chest-plate of Studdiness, Gauntlet of Taunting, "Oh dear," Lisa averts her gaze and Kari chuckles a little. Rivets sees neither wants to buy that one and tosses it nonchalantly over his shoulder, it makes a definitive clang when it lands.

The noise draws Lisa's attention to an object sitting behind Rivets, stuffed under the bench. A price tag hangs off it that reads 'Goggles, E', "What's that?" Lisa curiously points to the object. Rivets follows her finger and for a brief moment loses his smile. Then he cackles again, "That, deary, is goggles."

"What do they do?"

"Huh?"

"Well everything else you're selling is 'Something *of* Something', the tag just says 'Goggles'. So what do they do?"

"They protects yer eyes lassy. They's goggles."

"Protect your eyes from what?"

At this question Rivets leans in with a sideways look to the twins. They come closer to hear him whisper in a voice not any quieter than he was speaking before, "Lies, girls. They protects yer eyes from lies."

Lisa is intrigued and reaches for her pouch, "How much?"

"Oh no, no, no, Lassy. Yer can't afford 'em. Not you. Not a chance."

"What do you mean? I can easily afford this whole cart! How much for the goggles?"

"Read the tag, girl."

"It just says 'E'."

"'E' stands fer 'Everything'."

"Everything?" Lisa asks as Rivets nods his head, "What do you mean by 'everything'?"

"It's a simple concept, lassy. Everything. They cost everything yer got."

"Not on your life! That's unacceptable! Why would you even...?" Lisa is bewildered and a little angry, she is not used to not getting what she wants. Neither is Kari, "So you're telling us that those goofy looking eyeglass things..."

"Goggles."

"...goggles, are worth all that we own?!"

Rivets leans in again with a wicked smile, "That's the price, take 'em or leave 'em."

"Not a chance!" Kari grabs Lisa, who is still in shock at having her money turned down, and drags her back through the market square. Rivets goes back to his seat, folds his arms, and cracks a smile, "Told ye yer couldn't afford 'em."

#

By the time Everett has been brought across Lennenden River and dragged under the bridge, the group's leader has calmed down quite a bit. Enough, in fact, for a thought to cross his mind that brings him a swell of vengeful joy. The big one forces the young merchant to his knees before the wrath of the adventurers is halted, "Hang on there, Murk."

"What is it, Boss?" The large man is not used to stopping himself from killing something.

"I've had an idea." He strokes his chin as he looks at the helpless Master Brennem then back to his comrades, "You know what Renny's job was, right?"

"Yeah boss, he was bait. He stunk something awful, but he was good bait. He'd been baiting fer years. Hard to find a decent baitman these days."

"Exactly!" The boss points to Murk, "Exactly! Now Renny's gone we're gonna have to find another baitman." He smiles as a look of realisation creeps across the group, "I reckon we're going to be starting our auditions today." He leans in, placing his gruff and still bloodied face inches away from Everett's, "In fact, I reckon we've got our first applicant right here."

"Does...that mean you're not going to kill me?"

"Kill yer lad? Not a chance! We wouldn't dream of killing yer: takes away the purpose of being the bait."

"…Bait? What kind of bait?"

"The kind what gets us orcs. And, most likely, the kind what gets dead."

"Oh crap."

"Oh crap indeed, sonny. Get 'im to his feet and keep a hold of him. He's going to be coming with us today."

The group of adventurers organise themselves and bind Everett's hands together; Murk keeps a hold of the other end of the rope. The boss starts up again, "Seeing as you'll be joining us for the day I'd better introduce meself. My name's Jeff and this is Murk. The young lady is Mildred and this 'ere is Egger and Grayem. For the remainder of the day we will be your faithful companions. And you, you will be bait.

"C'mon crew, it's time to move out."

"Oh nooooooooooooooooo…" Everett Brennem, entirely unenthusiastic about his new career, finds himself exiting the city and heading north to the surrounding forest with a rowdy and excited group of adventurers determined to get their moneys-worth of entertainment out of him.

Chapter Three

"Told you that was a waste of time." Kari shoves Lisa as they walk away from the market square, "He's just a crazy old man who put one over on you."

"Why are you so upset? You're not the one who didn't get those goggles!"

"Why am I so upset? You mean besides getting hit on by an arrogant creep and getting dragged through a market full of sweaty morons?! Maybe because all I wanted to do was ride horses! But noooooo you had to go to market! So sure that he's hiding something! Well, now you know. He's just another idiot selling idiotic stuff to bigger idiots."

"But...those goggles..."

"Are. You. Serious!?"

"Kari, they were different from everything else. Hidden away. No claim of magic on them...just...goggles..."

Kari takes a hold of Lisa's sleeve and continues to pull her up the street, "You're in shock, Lisa. Getting your money turned away is messing with your brain."

"But why wouldn't he sell them?"

"Oh, I don't know...because he's crazy?! Now can we stop talking about those stupid goggles, get this smell out of our clothes, and go riding?"

"Okay, okay," Lisa brings her focus back to the present and sighs, "Let's go riding."

The girls make their way back up the fast filling streets, knowing their beautiful summer's day is going to be spent out in the fields and cliffs, breathing warm, clean air.

#

It must have rained in this part of the forest last night. Everett trudges along the trail, feet making an occasional sucking noise as he pulls them out of the mud. The group has been walking for about an hour and admiring the scenic surroundings: it is very nice. Lots of views over hills and cliffs, the forest promising mountains to the north, the undergrowth not too thick. The trail is becoming a bit more rugged, but besides that, Everett could easily enjoy this walk a lot. That is, if he weren't still tied up and being dragged along behind a group of people who want to see him die as orc-bait.

Besides that, the walk is absolutely beautiful.

The young merchant may not be a warrior, but he is not planning on letting them have an easy time of killing him. He's been working up his courage and has a very simple plan of escape. It starts by making sure he is walking behind the group, which he is. Murk still holds the rope, but only with one hand, so Everett seizes his moment. He winds up and kicks the large man as hard as he can between the legs. It has the desired effect. Murk buckles forward in surprised agony and lets go. Everett turns and runs, rolling up his bonds that are still keeping his hands tied.

He hears them crashing through the bush behind him, he may only have had a couple of seconds head start this time, but he is also a lot more sober. Everett leaps over fallen branches and down hills, he has no idea how to escape the skilled trackers he has infuriated, but he's going to give it his best shot.

Vaulting over a large rock he hits a mud patch on the landing and begins to slide down the hill. Attempting to correct himself, Everett stumbles and falls, the momentum carrying him quickly to a cliff's edge. His pursuers stop and stand on the rock to watch quizzically, as he unsuccessfully scrambles for a handhold, then looks up in panic before disappearing over the lip.

Everett falls through the air and hits a ledge about eight feet down; the momentum causes him to roll and catch his tied up hands on a protruding rock, leaving him dangling by his wrists over what feels like a very long way down.

A few seconds later five faces are staring down at him, "You lucky little git."

The ledge is no more than six feet wide, protruding about four feet from the cliff face. If he had slid off anywhere else...Everett looks over, yep that's a couple hundred extra feet of falling he would have been doing.

"Right. Mildred, go get our comrade and feel free to give him a bit of a kicking while you're at it."

"Yes boss."

"Then I'm sure Murk would like a word when he gets back up here."

"I sure would, boss." Murk is still trying to nurse his pain without making it look like he's nursing his pain.

Mildred makes the climb down to the ledge and grabs the loose end of the rope now hanging free. She is about to toss it up to Jeff when she stops in her tracks, "Er, boss?"

"Yes, Mildred?"

"You might want to get down here."

Jeff swings himself over and joins Mildred on the small platform. He stands in silence for a couple of seconds, then crouches down to speak to their hanging captive, "What was your name, Bait?"

"Uh, Everett? Everett Brennem."

"You ever pissed off a wizard, Everett?"

"Um. I don't think so."

"Got any magic in your family?"

"No..."

"Ever messed about with magical artifacts?"

"Not that I know of...why?"

"Because, young man, you seem to be emanatin' a whole lot of good luck. But judging by your own situation the good luck ain't for you." Jeff stands and then climbs back up before addressing the group, "Alright lads, get down there and help Mildred."

"But boss," Egger pipes up, "Mildred don't need no help getting Bait off that cliff."

"Forget about Bait, lad; he ain't going anywhere. There's a cave full o' someone's gold stash down there and we need to bury it somewhere different before the owner gets back."

They leave Everett hanging as the group gets to work emptying incredible riches out of a cave in the cliff face. It is extremely well hidden, invisible even, unless a person is standing directly on the ledge where Everett fell.

Master Brennem can hear whispered conversations about a...lucky charm?

#

The fields are a welcome relief from the busyness of the city and the smell of the market. The girls ride for the rest of the day; visiting their favourite spots under the trees and by the waterfalls, climbing rocks and jumping into the lake. Lisa's mind is elsewhere though, and even the setting sun reflecting glorious colours off the majestic White Rock Falls cannot get her attention. She has discovered the new feeling of not being able to have something she wants, and that has only made her want it more. She plans to negotiate, repeating the morning's adventure over and over in her mind - trying to think of some way to get Rivets to sell her the goggles. For a reasonable price.

Kari can see her sister's mind turning and is no fool. She knows exactly what is consuming Lisa's attention. Coming up with her own plan, Kari shakes her head, *The things I do for you, Lisa. You're going to owe me big time after this.*

They return to the stables just before dark and Kari sends Lisa back to the house, "Your mind really isn't here right now. I'll take care of the horses."

By 'take care of the horses' Kari means walk them into the stables so the stablehands can brush them, feed them, and make sure they're comfortable for the night. But Lisa happily lets Kari do this little extra work for her. Kari's plan is about to begin.

She passes the horses over to the stablehands and starts giving orders for the evening; the whole group of them begin rushing about to get everything done. They keep their heads down and get to work as quickly as possible. This is exactly what she was hoping for as she can now leave the stables and head down to market without anyone seeing.

#

The sun has almost disappeared by the time she gets there. Vendors are closing up shop and those with carts are all but gone. Rivets is just finishing packing up when Kari sees him. She keeps her distance and stays in the shadows to follow him as he makes his way back to Adayr. It is a few minutes before he reaches Lennenden river and the bridge that crosses it to connect the affluent with the common. It is not easy to stay hidden on the bridge, but fortunately Rivets has no reason to think he's being followed. Plus there are still enough people and carts for Kari to hide behind.

As they reach Adayr's port Kari notices that she stands out a lot in this part of town. Her clothes are a dead giveaway that she doesn't belong here and they immediately start to draw attention.

Seeing one girl staring at her, Kari quickly takes her by the arm into a side street, "I'll trade you." She whispers. The girl looks at her confused, "Trade what?"

"Clothes. Mine for yours. Hurry up and decide: I don't have long to wait."

It's an obvious choice for the poverty-stricken young woman, those clothes will fetch her enough food for a month. They make the exchange and Kari completes her disguise by rubbing mud on her face and in her hair. She looks over at the girl now in a beautiful riding dress, touching the silk of it with her fingers. Kari sees something she has never seen before - a human being. Just like herself. She aches a little as she recognises her great heartlessness. Smiling, she makes eye contact, "It looks good on you." Her counterpart blushes. Well, she probably blushes. It's hard to tell under all the dirt. Kari nods to say goodbye and gets her head back on mission. She emerges from the side street in peasant's rags, eyes and nose scrunched up at the stench they carry. Lisa is going to owe her big time for this.

Rushing back to where she last saw Rivets, it doesn't take long to find him; the old man isn't moving fast pulling that cart behind him. The evening is beginning in Adayr and that means the bars are starting to open, happy adventurers are finding their way to their favourite watering holes to share stories of the day's excitement. Kari weaves through them to keep Rivets in sight as he continues walking right through town.

In fact, Rivets goes a lot farther than Kari was expecting. She follows him for another twenty minutes into the farmland surrounding the city, there he takes a small dirt path to a tiny mud shack in the middle of some hedgerows. He lights a candle to see and empties the cart inside of his modest home. Kari waits in the dark a fair distance away until she sees the light go out; then she stands cautiously and musters her courage, *Here we go then.*

Moving as silently as she can, Kari carefully makes her way to the hut and crouches underneath a window. There is no glass, just a square hole cut through the wall. Taking a quick look inside she sees a room filled with junk; weapons, armour, and contraptions litter the floor and table. There is a mirror hanging on a door that leads to another room, she can only assume that is where Rivets is sleeping.

Kari lifts herself through the window and silently drops into the room. It is difficult to move in the darkness with so much to trip over, but she is surprised that her goal is not that hard to find. In fact the goggles are given pride of place on a shelf all by themselves.

Making her way across the room she takes them in her hand. They are weighty. Made of steel and leather and glass and rivets. Everything the man makes is covered in rivets. She smiles, this was much easier than she thought it was going to be. Looking over to the mirror she can't resist: Kari steps in front of the door to see herself all covered in dirt and rags, then smiles again as she carefully places the goggles on her head.

They are clear and clean, easy to see through, and kind of adventurer-looking. Proud with her evening of achievement, Kari turns to leave; but that is when the goggles do something very ungoggle-like. There is a flash of green and blue light that blinds her for a moment; it hurts her brain but she manages to stay silent. It is then that she hears movement coming from the other room.

Oh gods, Rivets is awake!

"Who's out there? I smells yer! I'm gonna put the whoopins on yer, so I am!"

Kari tries to get out of the room but Rivets is too fast. The bedroom door bursts open and there he stands with large club in hand, staring at Kari, who is wearing his goggles.

She looks at him and backs away in speechless terror. Tripping over a shield lying on the floor she scrambles, crawling backwards until connecting with the dirt wall. Through the eyes of the goggles she sees the old man as a fuzzy image, but that is not what is causing her heart to drop. The old man is a fuzzy image because the goggles pierce through the magical deception: he is not really there. What is really there is a very real, and very large, orc. Rivets looks at her with great sadness and pity, "Oh my child, you weren't ready to pay the price."

Kari manages to divert her fear to her legs, which emphatically agree with her brain that now would be the perfect time to leave. She leaps out of the window and sprints down the mud path, expecting a raging green monster to follow. But he doesn't.

It is not long before she gets back to town, and that is when her evening gets exponentially worse.

Chapter Four

Lisa has spent her evening pleasantly entertained with some books as she sits in the family library. She often rests here, hours swiftly disappearing as romance, adventure, and heroism dance through her imagination. She sighs, why can't real life heroes be more heroic, and less...sweaty?

It is strange, she realises, that although she came back to the house obsessed with the goggles she had seen on the cart this morning, for the last half an hour she has been able to read with very little distraction at all. In fact, she can barely remember what they look like.

"Lisa! Lisa!" A voice cries out through the library halls, "I know you're in here! Lisa!"

Lisa curiously puts her book down and pokes her head around the cubby hole she is curled up in. Seeing a filthy peasant girl running towards her past the great shelves is a disconcerting sight, and it is only her recognising Kari's terrified voice that keeps Lisa from fleeing this crazed visage.

And, ah, that's what the goggles look like.

"Lisa! We have to go! Now!" Kari reaches her sister and, grabbing her arm, tries to drag her back the way she came in.

Lisa is not sure yet about trusting this apparition that may just possibly be her sister, "Kari? Is that you?" Kari pulls the goggles off her face so that she can be seen properly. Lisa curls her nose up, "Why are you wearing those rags...and what is that smell?"

"There's no time to explain Lisa, we have to go!"

"You stole those goggles didn't you? Dad is going to be so angry!"

Pulling the offending article off her head, Kari holds them out for her sister, "I stole them for you, you great idiot! Here, put them on! Tell me what you see."

Lisa takes the goggles with a look of disgust: they haven't escaped the dirt smeared on Kari's face. Seeing the desperation in her sister's eyes, Lisa begrudgingly places the goggles over her head. Kari watches her expectantly as Lisa looks around through the clear glass, gazing quite unimpressed back at her, "Well...am I supposed to be seeing something?"

"You don't see it?"

"See what?"

Kari does not know what to do next. The goggles stopped working? That would be very poor timing, and a-typical of the day she's been having, "Lisa, you have to trust me, we need to leave...now."

"I'm not going anywhere with you looking like that. Or smelling like that."

"But, you don't understand..."

"You need to go clean up, and I need to go tell Dad what you've done. He'll be able to sort this mess out."

"Great idea! When you find him get him to come with you! We need to get out of here!"

"Forget it! I'm not going anywhere with you! You're acting crazy! Leave me alone!"

Seeing she is not going to have her way, and physically dragging Lisa out of the city will cause way too much commotion, Kari, still terrified, growls out in frustration as she forcibly reclaims the goggles from her sister, "Ow! Careful, you brat!"

Kari puts the goggles back on and yep, they still work, "Please, please come with me."

"Get lost," Lisa rubs her head, "I'm telling Dad."

Backing away a few steps Kari is at a loss for what to do. If Lisa won't believe her, there's no way her dad will. Giving one final pleading gesture, she begins to cry as she turns, fleeing the library and leaving her sister behind.

Lisa is slightly stunned as she watches Kari disappear. Still rubbing her sore head, she sighs and goes to pick up her books, "I'd better go tell Dad what's happened."

#

Kari runs down cobbled streets and past wealthy homes. A couple of minutes and she reaches the market but it is when, and only when, she crosses the bridge that she dares to look back. And there, laying beneath houses and market and mansions; invisible to everyone but herself as she stares through the magical lie, is a great, white dragon.

Kari finds the corner of an abandoned shack by the river to curl up against and cries quietly. She is exhausted, terrified, and very confused.

What is going on? What is that thing doing under all our houses? Is it really there? Are the goggles lying to me? Is Rivets really an orc?

Kari positions herself so she doesn't have to look across to Westport. Every now and then, however, she can't help but turn to see. Not wearing goggles, city built on hills. Wearing goggles, *City built on a freaking dragon!*

"I'm not going to hurt you."

The voice comes from the dark, towards the streets of Adayr. Kari can see no one, but the intonation is all too familiar. Calm and deep, it is the voice she heard in Rivets' hut. A rush of cold goes through her body and her eyes strain to see, she wishes they wouldn't try: Kari really doesn't want to see that thing again. She tries to speak in a calm and authoritative tone, "W-w-wha..?"

"I'm not going to hurt you."

Voice quaking with fear she asks, "What are you?"

"You saw."

"I don't want to see."

"Then I'll stay back here."

Kari hears someone sit down against the wall of a nearby building. Her ears have managed to pinpoint where the voice is coming from, but Rivets stays out of sight around the corner.

The old man, or orc, sighs with sadness, "It wasn't always like this, you know." Kari hears him settle in his seat, "We used to possess a magical gem that hid us from your kind. We were peaceful hunters who lived on the mountain slopes and wanted nothing to do with the outside world.

"We called this gem Rukktha and it was passed down through generations. She kept us safe by masking our existence so that when your kind saw us, you just saw humans. And we were content to be invisible.

"Then, just over a century ago, Rukktha was stolen from us. And all of a sudden we were found by you. We wondered if maybe you would want peace, but all you wanted was war. We couldn't understand why you were so violent toward us: we were not warriors. It was only when we finally found our precious Rukktha that it all made sense.

"Elves look very much like you, except they are taller with pointed ears. And they hate anything that does not match their standard of beauty. My people are strong, but we don't measure up in their eyes. They have hated and hunted us for centuries and are the reason we hid away in the first place. They found us, stole our precious gem, and rather than murder my people themselves, they convinced your kind to do their dirty work for them.

"They rule your city, disguised as humans, and pass laws that turn you into slaves to their will. It is highly likely that the leaders of your kind are in league with them."

Kari thinks of her father and then shakes her head. There is no way that he could know.

"We have found Rukktha, but we cannot get her back."

"Why not?"

"She lies in the very centre of Westport. Even I, as a Shaman, can only get as far as the market without being seen. The elf magic is too powerful for any orc to get close enough. Those goggles were our last hope for a peaceful resolution."

"What do you mean 'your last hope'?"

"I said 'our last hope'. Both our races. I crafted those goggles twenty years ago, infused with magic that would call to a human able to help our cause. And after twenty years of visiting that market every day, risking my life every day, they called to your sister and she sought them. But you stole them and they have become grafted to you. Your greed and recklessness have cost both our races dearly."

"But..."

"Child," Rivets is more sad than angry, "Do you think my people will just wait and let your kind continue to use us as trophies for hunting? They have been organising and training for years. I asked our chieftains for time to let the magic call but their patience is wearing thin. And now you have interfered with the magic on the eve of war. The dragon shall be woken.

Kari's heart drops once again, she is overwhelmed at what her actions may have wrought on the world, "The dragon?"

"Elves worship dragons. They see them as the pinnacle of creation. And dragons are lazy. This one has found the perfect hiding place. With Rukktha by its side it needs never move, just occasionally open its mouth so that elves can throw in my slaughtered people or misbehaving humans. But if war happens the dragon will wake, and that shall be a terrifying spectacle. If the stone is stolen, the dragon and the elves shall be exposed and the dragon shall also wake. But if the stone is shattered, your people have hope."

Kari's silence amply communicates her fear and confusion. Rivets attempts to explain, "The stone is affixed to the life force of the main thing it is hiding. If it is stolen then whatever it was hiding simply becomes visible again. But if it is shattered, the life force it is attached to is also shattered. Both shall die. The stone is connected to the life force of the dragon. If the gem is destroyed, so is the dragon.

"My people want Rukktha back. They want to hide away again. But it is too late for that: the world already knows us, and if we fail to steal it we may never get the chance again. The gem needs to be destroyed."

"How?"

"Unfortunately, girl, you have become the last hope of both our races. If you do not destroy the gem, countless lives shall be lost."

Kari gulps, "What do you want me to do?"

"The goggles you wear give you, and only you, the ability to see through the magic that masks your city. If I could have, I would have created goggles that could be used by anyone who wore them, but Rukktha is powerful magic and it took all my knowledge of the craft to create a tool that could accomplish this much." He grunts and shifts his weight, "With those goggles you must seek out Rukktha and then strike her with this." A green hand tosses a large war-hammer around the corner, which lands a couple of feet away from Kari, "When the gem on the hammer's end strikes Rukktha, she shall be destroyed and the dragon with her."

Kari shudders, "I don't know if I can."

"That is your choice. I sought out the chosen one, I have found the not-chosen one. A destiny thief. This was not your call, but you have stolen it and now the weight of it is yours. If you do not destroy the gem, your people shall all die. If you do destroy the gem, your people may still die. I have done all I can. Now you must do all you can."

Rivets stands to his feet, "One last thing, child. Rukktha will defend herself. She will show you visions in an attempt to protect herself from being destroyed. But as long as you wear the goggles you will see through them, just as you see through me.

"I wish you and your kind the best. I leave in the morning to return to my people."

As she hears Rivets' footsteps fade into the late evening streets, Kari timidly reaches for the long handle of the weapon that lays next to her. It is not as heavy as it looks: made of iron, rivets (of course), and on the striking end an orange gemstone. It lies within a leather strap designed to be attached over the back of the wearer. She weighs it in her hands, feeling the balance of it and the incredible responsibility that has been thrust on her. It is not an easy decision to make, but if she does nothing then she would bear the guilt of it for the rest of her life.

She sits for several minutes trying to wish away the thought that any of this is real, eventually reaching the conclusion that being remembered for trying is a better fate than being remembered for being too afraid. Wondering what on earth she is doing, Kari stands, straps the weapon over her back, and begins her walk back to Westport; shuddering every once in a while as fear mixes with the cool evening air.

I'm walking toward a dragon. I'm walking toward a dragon. I'm walking toward a freaking dragon.

#

Inside a familiar tavern once again, and still tied to Murk, Everett sits exhausted. Now fully sober, he watches the group celebrate their fantastic luck by getting entirely plastered. Jeff comes over laughing and slaps him on the back, "Who woulda thought! The kid has a cart full of crap, but the real magic he kept for himself! Never been so lucky in all my years, and all thanks to our new friend, Bait!" He staggers then slumps down in a chair next to Murk and the rest of his friends, "I thought for sure you'd die, ya little sod. But turns out you're our good luck charm!"

It had taken the rest of the day for the group to remove and re-bury whatever they couldn't carry with them. Then they made a point of returning to town and celebrating their brains out.

For Everett, his current situation brings quite the ambivalent feeling. On the one hand he is grateful to whichever deity answered his earlier prayers and kept him alive, on the other hand there is no way this group of lunatics is ever going to let him go if they assume he is some sort of lucky charm. And they aren't going to be sharing their find with him either. He needs to escape. For real this time. Then, if at all possible, work out a way to steal that gold.

It is another hour or so of drunken celebration before the young merchant gets his chance. Deftly lifting a knife from Jeff's belt he saws through the rope as they all watch Murk quaff his fifth flagon, foam covering his massive grinning face. Then Everett makes a run for it.

He gets outside and jumps on the first horse he finds, the shocked owner having the reins ripped from his grasp as the steed starts galloping toward the nearest city gate. Five stagger-ing angry drunks follow him outside and try to grab horses of their own. The owners are now prepared however, and resist the attempted thieving by starting a fight. A fight that is heard by the other patrons of the tavern, as well as several passers-by. Being the nature of a city occupied by adventurers, warriors, and mon-ster hunters, what started out as an honest bit of pursuit quickly becomes a full fledged brawl.

It is a few minutes before sheer determination allows Jeff and his group to escape the mass of enthusiastic violence and begin riding their newly acquired horses after their disappeared captive, "Shouf," Their leader tries hard to think clearly through his drunken haze, "He musht've went shouf. Comon.

"Lucky charm my arsh."

They leave the city and ride south after Everett, trusting very much in the horses to keep them in the right direction.

Chapter Five

Having crossed the bridge again Kari finds a building to hide behind and scans the scenery in an attempt to locate the gemstone. She is trying very hard not to look directly at the massive sleeping dragon. It isn't easy. Remembering that Rivets had said Rukktha is in the very centre of Westport, Kari makes her way through the silent streets. Knowing her city well she has a good idea about where she is going: in the very centre of Westport is where her father works: the courthouse. When she arrives there, however, she sees that completely surrounding the building, hugging it like a hot water bottle in winter time, is the scaled arm of a monster. Kari moves through the sleeping town to get a better look. It is very disconcerting to see the cobblestones of the streets underfoot transition into white scales.

The goggles seem drawn to magical energy, like they want to show Kari every trick that has been pulled over her eyes. She sees the magic layered with the real world all around her. It is unbalancing at first but she quickly adapts to seeing through buildings and comes to recognise the indistinct orange glow that surrounds every spell. The glow gets stronger the closer she comes to the courthouse. That, she reasons, must be the gemstone emanating all the magic.

Stopping at the street opposite, she eyes up the building. It is quite formidable and very real in its stone and mortar construction. What were once hills surrounding it have become a dragon's arm, leaving only one way into the building: right through the main doors. Her goggles reveal the magical power emanating from within.

There are two guards chatting on the front steps watching

the main approach. So heading to the front entrance in peasant's rags, carrying a war-hammer, might not get her inside. Well, not in the way she wants anyway.

*I can't turn back now. All humanity is relying on me...*she rolls her eyes and sighs, *No pressure Kari, just the fate of the world. Now, how to get inside.*

Readjusting the weapon on her back, Kari crosses the street and climbs the...

It's just a hill it's just a hill it's just a hill it's just a...

Having a higher vantage point she notices a window on the second floor has been left open a crack; probably letting some cool night air into relieve the summer heat. Kari smiles sarcastically to herself as she plans the climb to her second break and enter of the evening.

Growing up exploring the surrounding rocky hills has given her a good understanding of scaling obstacles; the climb to the second floor has several easy handholds and it proves to not be much effort. Peeking over the windowsill she sees a vacant office and pulls herself inside, quickly finding a shadowy corner to crouch herself down in. The magical glow is definitely stronger in the building, even covering objects that aren't spells. Kari makes her way to the door and opens it to spy out the adjoining hallway. Seeing no one she silently makes her way through, giving a quick look toward her father's office down the hall before continuing the search.

It is not that difficult to find her way closer to the gem: the magic gives it away to the goggles she wears. Getting ever brighter as she makes her way down the stairs of the empty courthouse and into the underground levels where the cells are. Unlike the upper section of the building, here there are definitely guards walking around and Kari is finding the war-hammer to be quite cumbersome in her search. It is hard to remain stealthy when the risk of clanging steel on stone is ever present. Finding a dimly-lit corner of the armoury, she rests it underneath some old shields so she can find the gem more easily, and return for the weapon when it is time to use it.

There are not many prisoners being held here; crime is incredibly rare in Westport and the crimes of Adayr tend to solve themselves with...disappearances. Adventurers don't take kindly to being stolen from, lied to, or having their friends killed. The cells of Westport are usually used to hold those wealthy citizens who have had too much to drink, but the occasional real criminal is held here for summary judgement and most often execution.

Tonight Kari finds herself sneaking past only two occupied cells filled with the snores of the intoxicated. The glow of magic surrounds her: she must be close now.

At the end of the hallway there is a large wooden door shut and locked against the stone walls. Creeping silently up to the keyhole Kari tries to look inside. The hole is, unfortunately, covered. Certain this must be the room, Kari heads back to look for the keys then pick up her war-hammer.

Anticipation starts to fill her nerves as Kari makes her way upstairs again to search for cell keys, mind racing with the possibilities of what she might see and what will happen when she destroys Rukktha. Unsure about what might be in the room, she starts to imagine all kinds of horrors the gem could show her to save itself from being destroyed. That is why she doesn't notice the guard in the hallway.

"Hey! You! I thought I smelled something in here. Stay right there!"

Kari does not stay right there. She does, in fact, run full tilt into the office room she first climbed into and then, for the second time this evening, exits her break and enter by jumping out the open window.

This window is slightly higher up than the last one however, and Kari finds herself grasping for a handhold on the stone wall. Managing to slow her descent, she still hits the ground with a painful thud. Cursing under her breath, Kari picks herself up and runs into Westport, hearing the shouting and clattering of guards behind her.

#

Phynel Williams rushes back to the courthouse, fear giving him an extra dose of speed. Lisa had met him at the door when he got home from work and told of Kari's latest misadventure. Phynel's heart filled with dread at the thought that, despite his best efforts to keep his children safe, they may have had such a great danger thrust upon them.

Knowledge may be powerful, but only if you are prepared for it. Losing his wife had taught him this valuable lesson and he had worked hard to keep his daughters from suffering the same fate.

Rushing past armed men that are scrambling and beginning to comb the streets, Phynel makes his way to the courthouse entrance where he is stopped by the pair of guards on duty, "I need to speak to Captain Lirethe, it's an emergency."

"Captain's rather busy at the moment, can it wait 'til morning?"

"It absolutely cannot I'm afraid. Is he in his office?"

"Far as I know, but he's got more pressing matters at hand right now, Mr. Williams. We just had a break in. The culprit's managed to escape, but we should have 'em in a few minutes. Then the Captain will be wanting to interrogate."

"Oh no." *Did Kari really go so far as to...?* "How did she get in?"

"Through a second story window. And how did you know it was a 'she'?"

"Because I think I know who it is. I need you to take me to the captain. Right now."

Phynel is escorted through the chaos and excitement of a courthouse in full emergency mode. It is rare that crime reaches this place, unheard of in Phynel's time of service, so the forces that are assigned here are buzzing with the hope of finally seeing some action. Even if it is just to chase down one intruder.

They reach a door which reads 'Captain Aren Lirethe'. The guard knocks to have his sergeant open for him. Bookcases fill every spare inch of the walls and a large desk occupies the far end of the room. Surrounding the desk are several officers poring over maps as they organise a plan to search the city.

"Not now, private. We don't have time for visitors. Mr. Williams, you can come back in the morning."

"Mr. Williams believes he knows who the interloper was, sergeant."

"Show him in." Captain Lirethe's voice is strong and easily heard from across the room.

The private leaves to return to his post as Phynel is escorted to the table by the sergeant. The six men standing wait for his statement, "Captain Lirethe, I have reason to believe I know who broke in here. However, due to the nature of tonight's events I request that this situation be treated in the highest form of secrecy. I would ask if you could only allow those with the highest security clearance to be in this room."

The captain pauses briefly before responding, "Mr. Williams, I trust that you are not exaggerating the seriousness of this situation."

"I don't believe I am, Captain."

"Very well." Captain Lirethe turns to two of the men, "Leave us."

"Yes sir."

Once they have left and the door has been shut, the captain remains with three of his officers. He motions for Phynel to sit across from him, "What is on your mind, Mr. Williams."

"Sir. I have come to beg for the life of my daughter."

#

With the war-hammer in the courthouse and the guards looking for her, there is no way Kari can see that she'll be able to get back in. There is only one hope she can think of, and it's a long stretch: Kari takes a zig-zagged route through the back alleys of the city and makes her way home to find Lisa.

Quickly searching through the house, Kari finds her pacing the floor in her bedroom. The shock that crosses her sister's face when Kari opens the door is briefly challenged by the look of disgust at the smell, before settling on worry. Kari watches these expressions with a hint of humour: she had forgotten about the rags and the dirt. Even the goggles are becoming comfortable enough to be ignored.

"What are you doing? Where have you been? What's going on?!" Lisa is very confused, "When I told Dad about you he looked terrified and ran off without a word! Why would he do that? What have you gotten yourself into? Kari, I'm scared! What's going on?!"

"You wouldn't believe me if I told you. But I think I know a way to help you understand." Kari grabs Lisa's sleeve, "Come with me."

"Are you kidding?" Lisa pulls back, "No! We're going to wait here for Dad to come back."

"Lisa, I'm leaving. And if you want to help anything at all you have to come with me." She lifts the goggles to show her pleading eyes; urgency in her voice, "Come on. Please! There's more at stake than you know."

"Yeah right. Like the world depends on you getting out of this house right now."

"......."

"Really?...No Kari, I'm not buying it."

"Please Lisa, I'm leaving now. And if you ever want to see me again, you need to come too." Kari turns and runs out the door, making her way to the stables outside. Lisa watches through the window as Kari mounts her horse, then growls in frustration before chasing after her sister: riding her own mount through the starless night.

#

Phynel remains seated across from Captain Lirethe, three officers standing around them. The pain he feels in his soul is more than evidenced on his face as he contemplates his encounter with Lisa, and the dread her words put in his heart. His tear-filled eyes are pleading, "Sir, I have lived these last twenty years serving this city. Serving you. When you allowed me to share the truth with my wife, I was so excited to be able to welcome her into the promise of such knowledge. How she reacted and the subsequent consequences taught me a valuable lesson, and I have spent these last seventeen years seeking to protect my daughters from that same fate. I declined to share the truth with them because of what happened to Julia." Phynel's voice starts to crack with sorrow,

"She was my love and I watched her taken away because of my naiveté in believing she was ready to know the truth. Since then I have been diligent in protecting my daughters. I would rather they remain unaware and happy, than risk them being taken away as she was. And that is why I am here. It terrifies me, but I think that someone may have forced Kari to see the truth. What I feared more than anything else is happening."

"You think Kari was the one who broke in here?"

"I do."

Captain Lirethe leans back in his chair, fingertips meeting in front of his mouth as he ponders this new information.

"I beg of you, give her a chance to listen to you. Give me a chance to speak with her. She will see that you have given us so much, and that it is for the betterment of our people that things remain as they are.

"Everything you have done for us has made this place better. Has made our race better. I am sure she will see this if we can just speak with her. Please Sir. Capture her, but give her a chance."

There is a pause as the captain deliberates Phynel's statement, "Mr. Williams. I understand this is a struggle for you, and I will do all I can for your daughter. But I am sure you understand that I cannot jeopardize the city or our operations for anyone. No matter how dear they may be to your heart." He leans forward on the desk, "I am also sure that message came across seventeen years ago.

"We will capture her, we will speak with her to ascertain what she knows, and from that point determine the best course of action.

"Now I highly recommend you tell us exactly what you know about where she is and why she is acting this way. I suggest you be accurate and thorough. For the sake of what remains of your family."

Chapter Six

Kari rides hard. With the guard looking for her she knows she has to avoid the city. Racing through the countryside to the north she circles around the farmlands that surround Westport and gallops toward Lennenden River. It is familiar ground that both Kari and her mount know well. Over her shoulder she can make out the silhouette of her sister in the darkness, barely keeping up but determined not to lose her. Seeing there may yet be hope, Kari smiles and pushes on.

The river crossing isn't easy; there is no bridge to traverse and the waters are untamed here. The horses have to swim through most of it and Kari is concerned not just about drowning, but also about making too much noise. It is silent at this part of the country and any noise can be heard from a fair distance. She hopes any farmers listening will just think it is coyotes or some similar wildlife. Mounting back up on the eastern shore she waits for Lisa to get a foothold before beginning to ride again. Lisa is too tired to object; resolving herself to the pursuit, she quickly gets back on her horse.

Kari leads her through more farmland before disappearing over a hill. Lisa pushes her horse even harder fearing Kari might lose her, but when she crests the hill she sees the horse left at the mouth of a small dirt trail leading into hedgerows. Lisa dismounts and cautiously begins treading into the darkness.

The silence is terrifying. Lisa has no idea where she is or where Kari might have gone to. The trail itself is well-worn and there are notches where a cart has, over the years, created deep grooves in the ground. Moving forward through the night Lisa comes upon the culprit cart and recognizes it immediately: Kari has led her to Rivets' home.

The place smells like mud and dung, making her shudder with the thought of what she may step or fall into, and then having to wear soiled clothes through the rest of this terrible misadventure. It is then that a hand appears from the bush and covers her mouth: dragging her to the ground. Looking up Lisa sees her sister, still wearing the goggles and with a finger to her lips signalling silence. Lisa nods and Kari lets go.

Kari is just as scared as Lisa. She doesn't know what is about to happen. Maybe Rivets will help, maybe he'll lose his temper. But she is mostly afraid of seeing him for what he truly is: a giant green monster. Giving a nod in the direction of the door Kari begins to move; Lisa grabs her sleeve and vehemently shakes her head. Kari raises the goggles to show her own fear and nods her head. This is the way it has to be. Lisa lets go and the pair of them silently step forward.

Kari hesitates, struggling to overcome her fear, then lightly taps on the rotten wood of the door. She whispers, "Rivets?" Kari really doesn't want him to hear her. There is no response so she tries again, knocking slightly harder this time and with a slightly louder, "Rivets?"

Nothing.

Kari swallows hard and grits her teeth. She gives a slight look back to make sure Lisa is still there and then gently pushes on the door. Its ominous creaking does nothing to help the sisters' mood as they crane their necks to stare at the darkness within.

Kari treads carefully into the hut, weapons and armour strewn about like so much detritus. There is a faint orange glow sitting throughout, residual magic she reasons, from the shaman's own masking spell, "Rivets?...Rivets? Are you here?"

Lisa steps in after her sister, eyes adjusting to the darkness of the single room. She sees all the scattered weapons, the mirror, and...the door. Both sisters look to one another and begin walking towards Rivets' bedroom.

"Why did you come here?"

The deep voice comes from behind them, neither girl dares

turn around.

"Rivets? Is that you?" Kari's voice is trembling once again.

"Turn and see, child."

"I don't want to."

"You are the one who came to my home. You either face me or I leave right now, and anything you want from me will be gone." His voice becomes stern, "Turn around."

The girls slowly turn to look back in the corner where Rivets now stands. Lisa sees an old man; Kari, a monster.

Thick set and tusked, removing the last of the weapons that had covered him moments before, Rivets hunches over to fit under the roof, "Why did you come here?"

"I…I need your help." Kari is almost crying she is so scared.

"I've already given all I can, child. I have set the path before you and given you hope. Use the hammer, save your people. Why did you bring her?"

"I…I…" she looks down, "I lost the hammer."

"Then you have lost your hope and your people are doomed. Not-Chosen One."

"But I have a plan! We can get it back. We can still save our people."

"I am not going back to that city. And you are not my people."

"Not you." Kari turns to Lisa, "Her."

"W-w-wait a minute!"

Kari turns her attention back to Rivets, "I need her to believe me. I need you to show her. I need you to tell her what's going on."

"Child, she is already terrified of this old man. And you want me to show her? What good will that do? You have lost the hammer; you have lost the city. My advice: take your sister and escape while you can."

"If she believes then she will help and we can still win! Please!"

"Child!" Rivets loses his calm demeanour for a second and the girls jump back, "No matter what happens, no one is going to win! This has nothing to do with anyone winning! I gave your people a chance and you stole it from them. That was your choice. That is your fate; Destiny Thief."

Kari begins to cry, "Please. Please help me. Please."

"Your tears mean nothing to me and they shall not sway me. Your people, your fate."

"Then why did you help?!" Kari finds courage beneath the tears and stares Rivets in the eyes, a couple of feet above the image of the old man, "All those years risking your life every day just to give us hope?! Then to throw us away like one of your fake weapons?!"

"You threw your hope away when you stole those goggles! You threw your hope away when you lost the hammer! It was you, girl. And only you."

"There is still hope! You said Lisa was the one the goggles chose; well, she's here. Help her to see!"

"Okay." Lisa is feeling very out of the loop, "See what? What is going on?!"

Rivets resignedly grunts and shrugs, "What do I care, I'm leaving anyway." Slowly the image of the old man fades away to reveal the reality of Rivets' frame. Lisa's eyes widen in amazement before blending into terror. Her scream is cut short by Kari tackling her to the ground and covering her mouth, she does not want any undue attention from random passers-by.

Rivets sits on the floor to join the girls as he tells the story of his people, and their fate at the hands of the elves. After a few minutes Kari doesn't have to hold Lisa down any longer. She removes the goggles and they both sit listening to the sad tale of a people mistreated and the hidden monster that laid the foundation of Westport a century ago.

Now that Lisa is finally listening, Kari tells her own story: her poor decision in stealing the goggles and her misfortune in losing the war-hammer, "But, I have a plan." She looks over at Lisa, "We can still save our people, if you help me."

"I-I don't know. This all seems way too much for us to do anything. I don't want to be in the middle of a war. And I definitely don't want to start one."

"Child," Rivets makes his way to his feet, "You did not start this war: it has already begun. Your choice will determine the fate of your people, just as mine has. Do all you can to destroy Rukktha. But if you fail, get out of the city. The dragon is going to wake." The orc shaman walks to the door, his disguise gradually cloaking him once again, "I wish you luck. May the gods grant you strength."

The door closes behind him and the two girls turn to stare at one another. A mixture of panic and adrenaline fills their hearts; combined with the overwhelming weight of responsibility that has been left at their inexperienced feet, one girl grits her teeth and steels her soul, the other shakes her head in fear, "No, no, no, no, no, no, no. I can't, Kari. I can't do this. I can't do this. I can't, Kari. No. I can't. I can't. I can't do this…"

"Hey, Lisa. Look at me. You can. We can. We have to. Just hear me out. We can do this, but I need your help. You can do this."

"I can't, I can't, I can't, I…"

"Listen to me." Kari takes her petrified sister by the shoulders, staring deep into her eyes, "Yes you can. You have to. I have a plan. Hear me out."

#

A few minutes later Lisa is galloping her horse back through the dawn streets of Adayr, tears in her eyes, "I can't do this, I can't do this. I can't. I just can't." Crossing the bridge to Westport she continues to cry in apprehension, pausing before entering the market square. Stopping for one last thought, fears and hopes wrestling in her mind, Lisa makes her decision and guides her horse to the courthouse.

The two guards are surprised to see someone riding toward the front gate so early in the morning, but wait for Lisa to dismount before addressing her, "Is that you, young Miss Williams? How can we help you this morning?"

"The girl who broke in here last night I…I know who she is. And…and I know where she is."

The guards give each other a glance, then one of them

ushers Lisa inside and guides her up the stairs. They pass several rooms before arriving at Captain Lirethe's closed door. The guard knocks and waits for the response, "Enter."

The door swings smoothly open, and Lisa is guided forward into a large room. Any other day she would be filled with wonder and asking to examine the books that fill the walls, but today... today she is very afraid.

She walks across the hardwood floor to a large desk at the far end of the room where two men sit. Three more stand around them. The one behind the desk is Captain Lirethe, but she is stunned and not a little concerned when the other seated man turns around. Lisa's father makes eye-contact with tear streaked face, his surprise mirroring her own. She continues to approach the desk with the guard, wondering what could possibly be going on. Maybe her dad is here for the same reason as her: with great concern for Kari and asking for help.

"Sir. Young lady here says she knows who broke in last night. Also says she knows where she is."

Captain Lirethe looks over to Lisa's father, "Leave us. Wait in your office."

Lisa watches her father stand slowly and look at her silently, "Daddy?" Pity in his bloodshot eyes, he puts his hand on her shoulder before walking out without saying a word. The guard exits with him.

The captain waits for the door to close before beckoning to the young woman, "Sit, please."

Lisa takes the now vacant chair across the desk and stares down, examining the wooden patterns and the maps of the city still laying over them.

Aren leans forward, "So, Miss Williams. Do you have something to tell me?"

Lisa pauses, working up the courage to get the words out, "You can't hurt her. Please. Promise me you won't hurt her. She's so confused and deceived. She needs help. Please. Please. She needs help..."

"Young lady, I will do everything in my power to help her.

But we need to find her first. Any information you are able to share will only make the process quicker and better for her. So please, tell me what you know."

Lisa tells him everything: Rivets, the goggles, the gemstone; Kari's fear and determination, her attempt to recruit Lisa, and the fact that Kari is going to try and break in again this morning. Lisa is in tears, "She's just so…delirious! I've never seen Kari like this. Those goggles have driven her mad. That orc has destroyed her mind. She thinks there's a dragon and every authority figure is some kind of magical enemy. You've got to help her, please!"

"Of course, Lisa, we want to help her. She's been attacked by a great evil and it sounds like her mind is becoming more and more lost. Did she tell you how she planned to break in again today?"

"She wanted me to go with her. She said…she said she needed my help."

Aren reaches across and gently puts his hand on her forearm, "Lisa, Kari does need your help. She needs you to help her be free of the magic that has taken hold of her. Please, for her sake, what is her plan?"

"…She…she's going to break in through the basement. Through the sewers. That orc had all kinds of weapons and tools and she's going to use them to cut her way in."

"Thank you, child. You have saved your sister, as well as your city. Please wait here: I have to collect her and prepare our people for an attack. I will return soon." Captain Lirethe stands and briskly walks out with his three officers, closing the door behind them. Lisa hears him call for guards and begin giving orders as his voice fades into the distance.

Waiting until she can no longer hear him, Lisa hurriedly moves to the other side of the desk. She opens the drawers but does not find what she is searching for. Looking around the room in desperation, she does not know what to do next: there is not much time. All she sees are the bookshelves filled with fascinating works. Checking through the desk again she crouches down to look inside the drawers. Noticing a small wooden lever within one of them, she gives it a pull. Lisa hears a catch release and turns to where the noise came from.

A section of the bookcase behind her has pivoted to reveal a hidden compartment. It is above her eye level but Lisa reaches up to feel for what she can find. A smile crosses her face as she pulls her hand back with the prize in her grip. Holding the key tightly she runs to the door and takes a deep breath, *Here we go then.*

Opening the door Lisa finds the hallway to be empty. The guards have been pulled from their stations in order to either find Kari or defend the city. Still anxious, however, Lisa cautiously makes her way down the stairs at the back of the courthouse. They lead to the basement were there is still quite a buzz of activity, with soldiers going through the armoury preparing for battle. She is forced to hide and wait in a quiet corner: it is several minutes before the basement has been emptied and the armoury is free to search.

Now, Kari had said that the war-hammer was hidden under some older, rusty shields. The room is quite large, but the recent flurry of activity has all but emptied it of the best weapons, leaving not a whole lot to search through. That is, unless one of the guards took the war-hammer to use. Lisa silently prays that is not the case as she hurriedly looks around, trying to move large pieces of equipment without making too much noise.

Thankfully the hammer is exactly where Kari left it, and exactly as Lisa had imagined it would look like. Large, powerful looking, and covered in rivets. She pulls it out of the sheath and hefts it in her hands, feeling the weight and balance. It feels surprisingly good to wield, and Lisa lets a small smile escape her lips: turns out she gets to be an adventurer like in the books she reads after all, and she doesn't even have to be one of the sweaty ones. Well, not that sweaty anyway. Silently exiting the armoury, Lisa makes her way to the dungeon below to finish her quest.

The walls are damp, cold stone and the cells are empty. The people Kari saw in them last night have apparently been released. Well, maybe been released. Lisa tries not to think about the other possibilities and runs with hammer in hand to the end of the hallway, where she finds the large wooden door. Heart beating through her chest with what she might see behind it, Lisa takes the key and puts it in the lock. The key turns smoothly and the door cracks open. She steps inside, not daring to look anywhere but the door that she locks behind her, leaving the key in the hole.

Kari had warned her of this moment. Whatever she sees when she turns around, no matter how horrific or how intimidating, she must strike it with the hammer. She must be brave. She must.

Lisa turns slowly, allowing her gaze to make its way gradually across the stone floor to the opposite end of the room. There, sitting with hands chained against the wall, is her sister.

Chapter Seven

Kari makes eye contact and gives a small painful smile from beneath her swollen lip. She is still in rags but the goggles have been taken, revealing a black eye that is fast swelling and a head wound that is bleeding down the right side of her face. Apparently she wasn't captured without a fight. She shifts her weight to find a more comfortable position, smiling with a hint of pride at her well-earned war wounds, "Hi Lisa."

Her voice is cracked and wounded as her face. There is blood in her mouth. Lisa walks slowly toward her, war-hammer ready to swing, "What happened, Kari?"

"They found me Lisa. They found me too fast." She looks down, "I'm sorry, I thought the plan would work. They put me in here and moved the stone. Rukktha is gone. We've failed. I've failed. I'm so sorry."

"You told me. You told me no matter what I saw in here, I had to destroy it. You told me..." Lisa's lip is trembling as she walks forward.

"I know I did. I know. And they know. That's why they put me in here. They want you to kill me. That is my punishment. And that is your punishment also."

Lisa is confused and afraid. She walks within striking distance and raises the war-hammer behind her, ready to swing, "How do I know that it's you? How can I know, Kari? I need to know."

Kari smiles reassuringly back up at her, "It's okay, Lisa. There's no way to know. The gem would show you a vision from your own mind; you wouldn't be able to tell the difference. If you swing I understand. If you don't, I'm still going to be chained here for the rest of my life. Which, if that invasion happens, won't be very long anyway."

"I...I don't know what to do."

"It's okay. I don't either."

Lisa's mind is racing. Kari had warned her about the stone and its power; that no matter what. No. Matter. What. She was to destroy whatever she found in this room. And here she is, hammer raised, about to swing and kill her own sister, with no way of knowing if she is a vision or the real thing.

Lisa desperately wants to do what is right but she does not know what that is, "I can't set you free. If you are the gem then the dragon will wake and kill everybody. You told me...you told me I have to..." She pulls the hammer back as Kari looks her in the eyes to nod and smile, letting her know it's okay.

Lisa tries to swing. She tries so hard. But she cannot overcome her own doubt. She tries, but she can't. She just can't. She lowers the weapon. If this really is Kari then she cannot kill her without destroying her own soul. She cannot kill her sister. She can't take that risk. She just can't. The tears fall as she collapses to her knees and puts her head in Kari's lap, "I'm sorry, I'm so sorry."

#

The tunnels beneath the courthouse are dark. There are no torches to line the walls down here, and no windows for any sunlight to break through. Kari is not troubled by this however: the magical aura surrounding the place lights up her eyes through the goggles, giving her near perfect vision.

She moves swiftly, leaving the broken stones behind where she penetrated from the sewers, along with the tools that got her through. Funny, she had always thought Rivets' creations were fake; turns out they come with instructions and actually work very well. That is, if you know what to do with them.

As she runs toward the opening ahead, she sees it is too late: the captain and three guards begin descending the ladder. Through the goggles Kari sees them for what they are, and is silently in awe of their beauty. Tall and strong, with sculpted faces and long hair. Eyes that are fired with colours and life, and long pointed ears that seem crafted only for elegance. Every move they make is pure grace. Kari stands briefly stunned before turning and running back the way she came.

The elves are quickly in pursuit. It is a matter of seconds before they catch her and restrain her against the wall, their grace being matched by their speed. Strong also, they hold her still as Alren speaks. His voice filled with contempt, "Well then, you pathetic creature. Your plan has failed. I'm half inclined to send you back to that orc, so you can die with the rest of his kind."

Kari struggles but is unable to break free. Glaring through the goggles she replies through clenched teeth, "I see you, elf! How can a being so blessed with beauty be so hideous? All that your kind has done…You disgust me."

The captain strikes her across the mouth, "You know nothing of disgust. Having to hide my form in order to live here, having to see such a pathetic visage of myself every day, just to get your stupid and ridiculous people to do what I tell them." He shudders with the thought, "But soon this episode of our existence will be over, and you shall join the other races beneath us as we serve the Great Ones. We have manipulated and controlled your people for over one hundred years; you have been our slaves, and soon you shall all realise it. And even then you will beg for slavery because of all that we offer you. Well, your kind will beg." He smirks, "You, however, shall be dead." He changes his tone to speak to the guards, "Take her to The Great One."

As the guards begin to move her, Alren gives one last jab.

"Your people are already slaves, and they love it. Do you want proof?" he pauses for dramatic affect, arrogant smile across his face, "Your own family told us how to find you."

Kari smiles back. She can't resist sticking one to the cocksure creature, "Are you sure that's what she did?"

The captain takes a step back, thoughtful concern crossing his face. Turning to one of the guards he orders, "Get her father and meet me at the gem. Move!" The two turn and run back to the ladder: disappearing to the levels above. The two guards left with Kari look to one another and begin walking her toward a side tunnel, "Should we take the goggles?"

"Oh, I don't think so," the reply comes behind a wicked smile, "She's going to want to see this."

#

Lisa jumps to her feet as the door rattles. The captain calls urgently, "Young Lisa! Are you in there? Let me in!"

Lisa looks down to her sister, "I don't know what to do, Kari. What are we going to do?"

"I don't know either, but whatever happens you need to get out of here alive. I'm already caught, we need you to be free."

The door starts to glow and hum with magical energy, then explodes. Lisa covers her sister, protecting her from the splinters and pieces of iron; when she turns she sees Captain Lirethe standing furious in the opening. Lisa quickly seizes the hammer and stands threatening to strike Kari, "Stay back! Or I'll swing! So help the gods I'll do it!"

The captain's sharp mind quickly evaluates the situation. He calms his demeanour, seeking to de-escalate what is in front of him, "No you won't, child. No, you won't. That is why I put her in here. There never was any gemstone: we keep this room for the most dangerous criminals. I wasn't sure if you had bought into the lies your sister had, so I needed to be sure."

"You were willing to risk her life?!"

"There was never any risk, child. From the moment you started speaking about her, I knew that you loved your sister with all your heart. You would never be able to kill her."

Alren starts to walk forward, "Stop where you are!" Lisa's voice commands his pace to halt: the weapon raised higher, Lisa's face a stone of defiance.

"Child," Alren's voice is silk on the air but his feet take no more steps, "If you kill your sister, your soul will be tortured for the rest of your life. Please," his pitying eyes gaze into her resolute glare, "Please put the weapon down."

#

"She'll do it! You'll see!" a struggling Kari is now being dragged further down the grim unlit tunnel, "She'll kill whatever monster that stone shows her! She's brave enough! She's strong enough!"

"Monster?" The one guard gives a brief grunt of humour, "She won't see a monster you fool. The gem protects itself by showing you the one thing you can't kill: the one thing you love most in the world. She won't be able to kill it because she won't be able to tell the difference. And she won't be able to take that risk."

"But you don't have to worry about that," the other elf pipes in, "You've got enough problems of your own. You know how we trade gold for orc carcasses? Ever wonder where all those bodies go? Well…" they round a corner to face a white stone wall, "You're about to find out."

The stones are not the truth; the goggles show her that as the wall begins to move. Anyone else here would only see pitch dark, but as the lips curl back Kari shudders and convulses in fear: the dragon's mouth opens for another morsel. She begins to struggle and flail in earnest as the guards have to fight her to continue their intent, "No!…No!…NO!!"

#

Lisa's father appears in the doorway behind the captain, the guard pushing him into the room, "Wh-what's going on?" Seeing his daughters in front of him he begins to run to them, "Oh, girls! What is happening?"

"Stay back! I'll swing this hammer, I swear!"

He stops. A look of panic on his face as he turns to Captain Lirethe, "You've got to help them! Please help them!"

"That is why you are here. I am of the firm belief that love can prevent disaster. I did not think that she would be capable of killing her sister but, it seems I may have been overconfident in their love. I need you to bring Lisa back to us." He looks sternly at their father, "I need you to prevent this from becoming a very bad day for your family."

The poor man turns to his daughters opposite in the large room; overcome with fear and sorrow, Phynel's voice quivers as he speaks, "Lisa? Honey? Everything is alright. Everything is… going to be alright."

#

Kari has broken free of their grasp and is fleeing the guards as she races back up the tunnel, desperate to help her sister. The elves are much faster than she and tackle her from behind, managing in the struggle to pin her with her back to the ground, "This would be a lot easier if we just killed her." The one guard begins to draw his sword, his eye is starting to swell from where he caught an elbow. The other one stops him, "Easier? Sure. But not nearly so much fun." Kari continues to struggle frantically, facing her beautifully horrific enemies, "I'm going to kill you! I'm going to kill both of you!"

The first guard rolls his eyes, "Fine, let's meet in the middle then." He takes her head and thrusts it against the stone floor, instantly stunning her into near unconsciousness, "See? Still alive. Now let's feed The Great One and get back to the captain."

They lift her by the arms and drag her back down the tunnel, Kari's head bobbing on her shoulders as she groggily tries to regain her strength.

The mouth opens again as the two elves begin gaining momentum, swinging her forward, "...no...please...no...please...no."

#

"Lisa. My dear, please. Please put down the hammer. Please. You don't want to do this."

"I don't, Daddy." Lisa's tears are streaming down her face, "I really don't. But I don't know what else to do. I'm so confused; please help me. Kari said I had to destroy whatever I found in this room."

"Honey, please don't swing that hammer. Please." Her father's tears match her own, "I already lost your mother to this city...please. I don't want to lose my daughters as well." He slowly steps toward her, pity and love pouring from his face, "Please. Put the weapon down. Come home with me." He holds out his hand, "Please. Come home with me."

Lisa lowers the hammer to waist height, lip trembling with sorrow, "Daddy, I want to go home." She sniffs as tears drip from her chin, weapon beginning to slip out of her grasp. She meets her father's gaze when a sudden wave of realisation comes upon her.

Lisa's eyes widen and her mouth opens in shock. Time becomes heavy as destiny grips the room.

Re-establishing her hold on the weapon, Lisa begins to swing. Her father jumps forward to stop her. Captain Lirethe sprints toward her. They are both too slow. Turning to see her sister's terrified gaze, Lisa powers the strike through her hips, creating a momentum that shatters the war-hammer on impact.

The gemstone explodes.

They are all thrown back by the release of magical energy; the ground cracks open and the walls collapse. The room is buried.

#

Kari feels a rush of floating as the two guards release her toward the dragon's open mouth, a rancid smell of brimstone and burnt flesh rising up from its gut. As the razored teeth draw closer she sees the bright pink and red of a giant tongue moving to snatch her out of the air. And then. An earthquake.

She watches the mouth and chin rear heavenward, mighty form uprooting buildings and landscape as a deafening scream echoes across the city. Passing through open space, Kari falls several feet before landing on a pile of golden artifacts warmed by the giant beast now flailing in agony above her. Still groggy and unable to move, Kari is at the mercy of the dragon and its death-throes. She smiles despite her situation, so very proud of her sister. Even without the goggles, she did it. She did it.

The dragon pushes away from Westport, plumes of flame roaring forth, sweeping land and sky. The beast desperately struggling for life, scattering buildings like shrapnel as she continues her flailing. People running and screaming, falling and dying, standing in shock as their city falls about them; gazing at the monster they never knew was there. A final agonising cry shakes the earth as the white-scaled giant collapses to its side, leaving the city a fiery ruin.

Kari lays still, stone and timber falling about her. It is a few minutes before the city stops quaking, but once it does, she finds herself thankful and a little surprised that she survived. It is a few minutes more before she is able to stand and begin her staggering trek to find her sister.

The streets are filled with panic. People run searching for their loved ones, others attack the now visible elves who are trying to regroup and fight back. Kari avoids as much of the mayhem as she can and pushes her way to where the gemstone was held. Seeing the courthouse in ruins Kari begins to run, "Oh, no. Oh, no, no, no, no, no…"

She makes her way through the rubble, digging and pushing the stones as much as she can in her frantic state, "No, no, no, no, no, no, no, no, no, Lisa, please no." But that is not who she finds. Her father's lifeless form lies prostate on the cracked ground. Shock overwhelms her heart and she falls on his body, "Daddy?… Daddy! No!…no…" The tears begin to fall across her dirt-stained face and her lips tremble with sorrow, "Daddy, why? Why? Daddy, why?" Her confusion and grief begin to break her heart.

"Kari?" Her sister's voice is weak, almost a whisper. Recognising it immediately Kari pulls her mind back to the present. Jumping over a large stone she finds a rafter has protected Lisa's face and body from much of the devastation that surrounds. Lisa's legs, however, lie under rubble. They are crushed and her life is fast fading.

"I'm here, I'm here, it's me." Kari cradles Lisa's head as she tries to comfort her.

"I did it, didn't I?" Lisa smiles up at her tearful sister, "I killed the dragon."

"You did." Kari is struggling to hold back her sobbing, "You really did." Lisa gives a brief laugh, "I'm a dragon slayer." Kari smiles back, "Yes you are."

Seeing the distress in Kari's eyes, Lisa reaches up and wipes a tear off her sister's cheek, "Still wearing those googles, huh? It was you, you know. It was you. The stone showed me you. It read my heart and showed me the thing I love most in the whole world. And it showed me you. I love you, Kari."

Pulling the goggles off her head, Kari lets them drop to the ground, "I love you too, Lisa." She bursts into tears and hugs her prone sister tight, "Don't go, okay? Don't go. Stay with me. Please stay."

"It's okay. It's going to be okay. Live a good life, Kari. Do that for me?" Sniffing back her bawling, Kari responds, "I will. I will, I promise. You're going to live it with me."

"Dear sister, we both know what is happening. It's okay." Lisa pushes back to see Kari's face, "It's okay."

Kari doesn't respond, she grips her sister tightly once again and continues to cry into her shoulder before pausing and pulling back a little, "How did you know? When you swung the hammer? How did you know it wasn't me?" Lisa chuckles a little in response, so glad that Kari asked, "Dear sister," Lisa smiles at her confused face, "Kari. She didn't stink."

They both laugh and hug one another through tears, Lisa getting weaker each second, "I'm going to miss you, Kari. I love you. Be good."

"No, no, no, no, no, no, no, no, stay with me. Stay with me." Kari's voice is frantic as Lisa exhales and her body slowly becomes limp, "Stay with me. Stay with me, Lisa! Stay!"

But she is gone. Kari wails as she holds her sister tight, weeping over her lifeless form; the love, the memories, and the dreams that will never be known.

She sits for hours, the chaos of the city passing around like a reflection in a pond. Humans and elves, warring and screaming, it is all blurred dreams passing around her from memory to shadow. The only reality is a rising anger deep within her soul. A resolve that starts to overtake every part of her. A hatred that floods every thought until Kari stands, resolved to one task alone.

I'm going to hunt down every elf. Every orc. Every thing *that has caused my family to die and I am going to kill it.*

She reaches for the goggles and puts them back on her head. Fuelled by pure hatred Kari makes her way out of the city; intent on spending the rest of her life wreaking vengeance for the pain that has been poured out on her heart. She disappears into the surrounding forest, searching for other, likeminded souls.

#

Jeff stands next to his horse. Mouth agape and eyes fixed forward. A look of shock and puzzlement frozen on his face.

"Huh."

The group has dismounted and stand dumbfounded next to him, staring at the devastation of Adayr from a distant hill. Everett drops from the back of the horse he is laying across and lands uncomfortably in the dirt. Bound hand and foot, it takes him a few seconds of shuffling his body around before he can take in the view that has left his captors speechless.

Westport's rubble burns in the morning sun, a great white dragon lays dead west of where the city used to be, screams and fighting can be heard coming from the survivors, and crowds of people can be seen heading toward them on the south road.

"Boss?"

"Yes, Egger?"

"What…?"

"I dunno, Egger."

"But how…"

"Not a sodding clue."

"We've got to get our money before this gets worse!" Mildred starts to make for the road.

"Hold up, lass," Jeff grabs her by the shoulder, "None of us are going into that."

"Why not? We need our sodding money!"

Jeff pulls her close to point at the city, "We're not going into that," He moves his arm, directing everyone's attention to the east, "because of that."

'That' happens to be a massive green swathe moving rapidly toward the city. An army of enraged orcs rushing forward with murderous intent.

"Point taken."

"What gets me though, is this." Jeff turns to look at Everett, "If he hadn't of legged it, we would currently be down there and, most probably, be dead."

Jeff lifts Everett to his feet and looks him up and down, "Y'know, I was starting to doubt, but I think you might just be a lucky charm after all. Either way, I think we'll be keeping you 'round 'til you prove otherwise."

"What're we gonna do now, Boss?"

"We've got to head south, Grayem. Let people know what happened. Respond in kind."

"What did happen?"

"I don't have a sodding clue."

Epilogue

A matter of hours after the dragon dies, the invasion begins. The orc horde swiftly moves through the city of Adayr, crossing into the ruins of Westport the same day. There is too much confusion for there to be any resistance. Most of the occupants flee, the rest die.

As the sun begins to set, a single orc makes his way through the rubble. Ignoring the chaos and celebration that occurs after battle, he searches for the hero of the day.

Rivets stands over the body of Lisa, his large green arms easily removing the stones that lay upon her. When he is done, he looks down to see her crushed legs and shakes his head, "For what it is worth child, thank you."

He reaches for the bow that is strapped to his back and puts an arrow on the string, "All of my weapons worked, you know," He draws it back and takes aim at the lifeless body, "You humans just never read the instructions."

He lets the arrow fly.

* * *

Manufactured by Amazon.ca
Bolton, ON

10432457R00037